Paying It Forward, Skyler-Style

Ruth McDonald Mair

Editor: Tracy Ruckman

Illustrator: Ashleigh E. Houska

ISBN-13: 978-1507655641

In loving memory of Skyler Swain.

Dedicated to all the young angels who will live forever in our hearts, including:

Creigh Patrick Bisson

Jonathan Harris Burkett

Nicholas W. Greenhoe

Brianna Nicole Heeney

David Frank John Mair

Justin "JP" Proper

Nash Gregory Schupbach

Michael Gregory Edward Stewart

Skyler James Swain

Alex was sitting on the steps in front of his house one summer afternoon. He was kind of sad because he was missing his friend, Skyler, who, after being very sick for a long time had recently gone to live in Heaven to help Jesus.

Alex's older sister, Liz, came running out the door, and she was not in a good mood. "Get out of my way, Alex! I am late for my piano lesson." As she tried to rush past Alex, she bumped into him and dropped the practice music for her piano lesson. The pages scattered all over on the ground. "Oh Alex, I am going to be so late and Mrs. Ellison is going to be so mad! You know she doesn't like it when her students are late for lessons."

"It's okay, Liz. I will help you pick up your practice music so you won't be late." Alex handed the pages to Liz.

Liz looked at her brother and said, "Gee Alex, I am so sorry I snapped at you. It isn't your fault that I dropped my music. I should have been ready to go earlier."

Alex said, "Don't worry about it. I was just sitting here thinking about Skyler and how he always liked helping someone out and making them smile. I guess I helped you out Skyler-style today."

As Liz was walking up the sidewalk just on time for her piano lesson, Mrs. Ellison was plucking at a few weeds from the flowers by the door. "Hi Liz! I am so glad you could make it for your lesson today. I was just pulling a few weeds while Mr. Ellison is sick. I have been taking care of him and haven't had time to care for the lawn. Mr. Ellison says that when he is better in a few days he will take care of it. Come on in for your lesson. I can't wait to hear you play the music I gave you last week!"

All the way home from her piano lesson, Liz though about Mr. and Mrs. Ellison. That night at dinner, she tol her parents that Mr. Ellison had been sick and unable to d work around the house. She said that if they didn't mind she would like to go over and help Mr. and Mrs. Ellison th next day. Liz's parents both agreed that was a wonderfu idea. Liz's dad said, "I will go, too. I will mow the lawn whil you pull the weeds that are in the flowers."

As Liz's dad placed the ham on the table her mom said, "I will make some soup and a pie for you to take t them."

The next day, Liz and her dad headed over to Mr. and Mrs. Ellison's house. They hadn't told the Ellisons they were coming, and when they arrived, Mr. and Mrs. Ellison were not at home. Liz started pulling weeds from the flowerbeds while her dad mowed the lawn. Just as they were finishing, the Ellisons pulled in the driveway.

"Oh my goodness!" exclaimed Mrs. Ellison. "Liz, it was so nice of you and your dad to do this for us. What do I owe you?"

"You don't owe us anything," Liz told her. "We wanted to help. My mom also sent some soup and an apple pie over for the two of you to enjoy. My brother, Alex, helped me out yesterday, so I guess you could say we are paying it forward, Skyler-style." Liz explained to Mr. and Mrs. Ellison about Alex's friend and how he always was so helpful and cheerful.

They each hugged Liz, shook her dad's hand and thanked them again for helping them get their yard work done.

The next day, Mrs. Ellison was in the store to pick up a few groceries for the coming week. Waiting in line at the cash register, she heard the lady in front of her ask the cashier to put a few of the items off to the side because she didn't bring enough money with her. Mrs. Ellison had seen the lady in the store before and recalled someone calling her "Cindy." Mrs. Ellison touched the woman's arm and said "Excuse me, Cindy, but I would like to pay for your groceries today." Mrs. Ellison told the cashier to total up Cindy's groceries and hers together.

Cindy looked at Mrs. Ellison and said, "Thank you so much. How can I ever repay you?"

Mrs. Ellison smiled at her and told her the story of Skyler and asked her to just pay it forward Skyler-style.

Later that week, Cindy decided to pick up dinner for her family on the way home from work. She placed her order and pulled up to the window to pay. The cashier asked if there was anything else she needed. Cindy realized that this was a good time for her to pay it forward Skyler style, so she told the cashier that she wanted to pay for the food for the people in the car behind her. The cashier said, "That's very nice of you! Do you know them?" Cindy answered that she did not know them and to just tell them to pay it forward Skyler-style when they had a chance. She paid for all the food and headed home with a warm feeling in her heart.

On Saturday, Alex and his mom decided to walk to the park since it was such a nice day. They were sitting on a bench with another man in the park, watching people walk by and talking about what a good friend Skyler had been, not only to Alex, but to everyone he met. Alex said that he knew Skyler was in heaven helping Jesus now.

Suddenly, Alex heard the sound of the music from the ice cream truck. He jumped up from the bench and reached into his pocket. He pulled the change out of his pocket and counted it. "Nine cents," said Alex as he looked as his mom. "I can't get any ice cream today, I guess."

His mom looked at him and said, "Since we walked to the park today I didn't bring my purse so I don't have any money with me either." Alex sat back down and watched as the man who had been sitting next to him walked up to the ice cream truck and bought a chocolate and vanilla swirl ice cream cone—Alex's favorite!

The man walked back toward the bench, but instead of sitting back down, he walked up to Alex and said, "Hello. My name is Paul. I went to a drive-thru with my family the other night and the person in front of me paid for my food and told the cashier to tell me to just pay it forward Skyler-style when I had a chance. I had no clue what that meant until I overheard you and your mom talking about your friend, Skyler. When I saw that you did not have enough money with you to buy an ice cream, I decided this was a perfect opportunity to pay it forward. I hope the flavor is one you like."

Alex's eyes grew large and he got a huge smile on his face as he said, "Chocolate and vanilla swirl is my favorite!" Then he turned to his mom and asked, "Is it ok, mom?" His mom nodded. As Paul sat back down on the bench, he asked Alex to tell him more about Skyler. So while Alex enjoyed his ice cream he told Paul all about Skyler and how he had always managed to make someone smile, and if he noticed someone was particularly sad, he would try that much harder to make them smile. Paul looked at Alex and said, "I am glad you had such a good friend. Let's make a deal to always keep paying it forward, Skyler-style!"

42750872R00018

Made in the USA
Middletown, DE
21 April 2017